CW00519821

Copyright© i2f Publishing. 2021
First Published 2021©Howard Wright

The right of Howard Wright to be identified as the author of this work has been asserted by him in accordance with the Copyright, Designs and Patents Act of 1998.

ISBN 978-0-9563617-3-8

British Library Cataloguing-in-Publication Data
A catalogue record for this book is a available from the British Library

The Rats of Eyam

A children's story of the plague in Eyam in 1666,
this time from the village Rats perspective

With thanks to the children of years 5 & 6 at Eyam Primary School for their illustrations which I have used throughout the book.

Contents

Life in the Graveyard

April 1665

Whiskers, Scratch, and Snitch are three rats that live in an old rotten log in the graveyard of the St Lawrence church in the small village of Eyam in Derbyshire.

Whiskers and Scratch are small brown rats with relatively short tails, but Snitch is a huge grey rat with a long tail, huge teeth, and great big feet.

His feet are so big that sometimes he accidentally steps on his friends. He always must always be careful. "Watch out, Snitch!" Scratch would shout.

It has been a cold hard winter, and food is in short supply. Many households are finding it hard to survive, so any scraps of food that are left are being used, leaving nothing for the rats to eat.

Snow is covering the ground, and it is so cold that all the rivers and ponds have frozen over with a thick layer of ice.

"I'm so hungry," Scratch complained. "We haven't had anything to eat for days. My tummy is grumbling all the time."

"I'm hungry too," Whiskers whined. "Snitch, why don't you go out and find some food. "Your eyes are bigger, so you can see better than us, and with your big paws and mouth, you can carry more food."

"Being bigger makes it easier for cats, dogs, and foxes to see me," Snitch replied.

"Be careful. Make sure you don't let them see you, and if they do, kick them with your big feet!," Scratch giggled.

"That's not funny," Snitch pouted. "I'll go, but don't be surprised if I don't come back. Everyone is hungry at this time of year; if we're hungry, so are the foxes, dogs, and cats so they will all be after me!."

Snitch carefully left the graveyard after it went dark and plodded through the snow. Snitch's big feet are constantly tripping him up. "Brrrr. I'm freezing," he says, rubbing his paws together. He walked and walked and soon came upon a small cottage on the edge of the village by the woods.

He saw smoke coming out of the cottage chimney. "It looks like they may have food in there." He sniffed

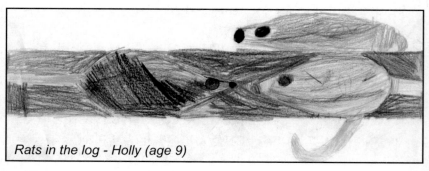

Rats in the log - Holly (age 9)

the air. "Smells like soup. It's probably bubbling away in a big iron pot over an open fire- I can just image it.

Mmmmm." Snitch's tummy rumbled with hunger.

He crept closer and closer to the cottage, always on the lookout for danger.

As he gets close to the cottage, the front door suddenly opens wide, and a shabbily dressed man ambles out and looks around. He picks up a few of the pieces of the wood that are piled by the side of the door and turns to go back in.

Before he can close the door Snitch dashes through his legs, "This is my chance!," Snitch thought.

As Snitch runs into the cottage, the door slams shut behind him with a clunk, nearly trapping his long tail.

Snitch scuttles across the floor and quickly dashes under an old chair, crouching down he sits and gets his breath back. "It's so warm in here," he says, rubbing his paws and enjoying the heat.

After a few minutes, he thinks, "I'll have a look and see if I can find anything to eat."

Carefully he creeps out from under the chair.

"Mmm, there's the fire with the cooking pot above it and it smells like there may be bread in the oven".

Snitch looks around the cottage and sees that in the other corner of the room, on a chair is the biggest ginger cat he has ever seen.

Oh no! It's a cat." He gulps and quickly runs back behind the chair.

The big ginger cat looks around lazily and sniffs the air. He's clearly a lazy cat as his eyes slowly close, and he wraps his tail back around his head and dozes back to sleep.

Snitch decides to wait a while to make sure the cat is really asleep, but after a time, his tummy is growling so loudly that he is convinced the cat will hear it.

Snitch pokes his stomach with his paws, hoping that it might stop it from making such a noise, but it doesn't, and it just keeps rumbling.

He thinks of his friends, Scratch, and Whiskers and knows they must be even hungrier than he is.

"I've got to get some food!" He says to himself. He peeks around the edge of the chair again and sees that the cat is sleeping soundly.

Slowly he creeps from behind the chair and heads towards the fire in the kitchen. There is a pot of soup bubbling away over the fire. "Yummy," he whispers to himself. But he cant get at it because it is too high and the fire is so hot.

He turns round and looks at the table in the middle of the room. "There is bound to be something on there" he thinks.

Snitch scampers up the table leg on to the table. He spots a plate piled high with hot toast and bacon that smelt delicious. He licked his lips "that looks good," he says and as there was nobody around he runs across to the plate and begins to chew on a piece of bacon.

He is just enjoying the glorious taste of the bacon when suddenly he jumps. Someone has clearly seen him as he hears - "SHRIEK! SHRIEK! SHRIEK!"

"It's a rat, and it's on our kitchen table!" A small round woman has come down the stairs into the kitchen. She rushes across to the chair where the cat is sleeping and shouts. "Tom, wake up you lazy cat, get on with you and catch the rat!".

Snitch gulps in terror. He freezes in fear as the big ginger cat yawns and jumps off the chair. It moves slowly towards him, its eyes fix on him. The cats tail is twitches and it gets ready to pounce. It creeps slowly towards Snitch.

"Yikes!" shrieks Snitch, panicking; he quickly grabs a slice of bacon in his mouth and runs down the leg of the table, across the living room floor, and hides under the chair again.

The cat chases him and pounces. Luckily for Snitch, it catches its claws in the material draped over the chair. MEOW it cries as it struggles to get its claws untangled.

Just then there is a knock at the door, and the door opens and a tall thin man puts his head round the door and shouts "are you there Richard - what's all the noise?".

"Come in quickly the" cottage owner says, "we've got a rat in here and the stupid lazy cat is trying to catch it.

The visitor walks into the cottage and starts to close the door behind him. But before the door is about to close, Snitch takes the opportunity and dashes through the visitors' legs and out through the open door.

As he gets outside, he hears the door slam behind him and he looks round to see if the cat is still after him. All he can hear though is the mournful meowing of the cat as it tries to get untangled. But it is too late the door had shut and the cat cant get out.

Snitch turns around and runs as fast as he can to get away from the cottage before the cat gets free and is let out of the door.

He runs back towards village as fast as he can and as he gets close to the graveyard, he finds a large pile of grass at the side of a wall and crawls inside. He sits there shivering; his heart pounding with the excitement and the fear of the last few minutes.

"Where's the bacon?" Snitch wonders. "Oh no, I must have dropped it. I am certainly not going back for it now," he frowns.

Once he calms down and his heart stops pounding, he listens, and when he is sure that there is no cat around, He slowly comes out of the grass, sniffing the air to see if he can still smell the cat.

The coast seems to be clear and thankfully the cat is nowhere to be seen. But he has nothing to take back to his friends as he has dropped the piece of bacon he stole.

"I am going to have to find something to take back to Whiskers and Scratch" he says to himself.

Luckily for him, lying near one of the graves are some flower seeds. "I guess this will have to do." He carefully picks them up in his mouth, storing them in his cheeks and runs home to the log.

"Where have you been?" Whiskers asks.

"We thought a cat or a fox must have eaten you," Scratch says.

"It nearly did," Snitch gulps. He tells his friends what has happened. How he sneaked into the cottage and how the enormous ginger cat pounced on him.

"I was lucky to get away - if the visitor hadn't come to see what all the noise was I wouldn't be here now. Luckily the door had slammed shut and I managed to get out before the cat had got itself untangled. But all I have for you are these few flower seeds."

"That's good enough for me," Whiskers says.

"Me too," Scratch added.

The three rats shivered in the cold and Scratch and Whiskers nibble on their seeds, happy that at least they have some food. When all the seeds have been eaten the three rats curl up together in a heap at the back of the log to keep warm. They doze off to sleep thankful that they don't have to worry about Tom, the cat eating them!

The Stocks

June 1665

One sunny morning Snitch yawns and says, "I am so hungry I'm going to go up to the Stocks on the village green to see if there is anything up there to eat. If someone has been bad, they usually put them in the stocks and throw fruit or vegetables at them, so it can be a good place to find food".

"Be careful," says Scratch, "the last time I was there, I nearly got eaten by a great big dog."

Snitch washes his whiskers and heads out of the log. As he goes he waves goodbye and trots off through the graveyard and heading up the street to the village green where the stocks are. To make sure he is not seen he stays in the grass and keeps close to the wall.

When he gets close to the stocks, he stops quickly and hides behind a wall. At the stocks there is another group of scruffy-looking rats snuffling around looking for food.

The biggest of the rats sniffs the air and turns. It

Snitch and hisses "What do you want,"

"Just looking for something to eat for my friends," says Snitch.

"Well, clear off," says the rat, "This is our territory, and anything that's left here is ours."

"Who says so" snarls Snitch standing up on his back feet to make himself look bigger.

"We do," choruses the group of rats and they gather round and menacingly move towards Snitch.

As Snitch is so hungry, he decides to take a chance, and runs as fast as he can to the stocks and grabs half an apple in his jaws, turns and run back towards the churchyard.

The biggest of the other rats snarls and lashes out at Snitch with his claws as he dashes past.

He catches Snitch on his ear, which draws blood. Snitch yelps and tumbles onto his back as he is caught off guard. He quickly scrabbles to his feet, rubs the blood from his eye and moves slowly towards the wall - careful not to turn his back on the other rats.

"Get away from here and don't come back," snarls the biggest of the rats.

The other rats gather behind their leader, and Snitch takes one look and decides that he doesn't stand a chance if there was a fight.

He still has the piece of apple in his mouth, so he thinks, "Let me get away from here as quick as I can."

He sets off running as fast as he can back down the high street towards the church.

The other rats start to chase him, but they soon become tired and slow down, turn, and head back to the stocks.

When he sees that they have turned he stops and hides under a bush at the side of the road. "Phew, that's was a bit too close," he thinks.

Rats at the stocks - Katherine (age 10)

He is happy, though, as he at least has a piece of apple for him and his friends to share.

Snitch scurries back down the village towards the graveyard - making sure he keeps in the grass by side of the road so he isn't seen.

When he gets back to the log, he puts the apple down and the three rats start to eat. After a few minutes when the apple has finished Snitch says, "Wow, that was really bad, there is a group of rats I have not seen before up at the stocks and they are really viscous."

Whiskers notices that there is dried blood on Snitch's head, "Where has that blood come from" he asks.

"The leader of the rats took a swipe at me and caught my ear," Snitch winces as he wipes it with his paw.

Scratch comes over to him and licks the blood which is running down his face, "it looks worse than it is," he says.

I don't think we should go up there again", says Whiskers, "I know we're hungry, but I would rather find food in the hedges and fields rather than risking a fight with those rats again."

Snitch says "Were well hidden here in this old log and few people visit this part of the graveyard.

"I like living here in the graveyard", says Whiskers, "nobody bothers us," .

"Yes, we are lucky," says Scratch

Let's hope it stays that way," says Snitch yawning and the three of them curl up in the back of the log and go to sleep.

Rats in their log - Hannah - (age 11)

Scratch, Scratch, Scratch

But is there ever a dog that praised his fleas?
William Butler Yeats

September 1665

After a warm spring, the summer brings warmer weather, the trees are full of berries and there are plenty seeds in the fields. It's a welcome change for the graveyard rats as there is plenty for the rats to eat without risking going into the village.

It is the same for the inhabitants of Eyam as the villagers start to harvest their vegetables, potatoes to provide food for the coming months. Being a small village, they have to provide most of the food for themselves.

The village is busy as usual, with people bustling around the streets. There is always lots happening, and the village has many visitors bringing food and other wares to sell and exchange.

The main way into the village, the Lydgate, a steep road from Stoney Middleton, the next village.

The road is usually busy and there are always

scraps of food dropped by travellers as they make their way to the village. This is a good source of food for the rats and it is a daily routine for the rats to patrol the edges of the road gathering what they can.

It is a warm morning when the rats head out looking for food on the Lydgate but there is very little and the road is unusually quiet.

As there is nothing to eat by the road the three rats head back towards the graveyard. Whiskers decides he will go into the village and look for food in and around the houses.

After a while he comes back to the log and puts down a few scraps of food on the floor. The three rats greedily tuck in.

As they are eating, Whiskers suddenly stops and starts scratching frantically behind his ear.

 "What are you doing?" asks Scratch, "That's what I usually do.

"Where did you find this food?", asks Snitch.

Whiskers says, "I got this at the back of one of the houses by the church"

"Just before that I went up to the tailor's cottage to see if there are any food scraps up there, I went through the crack in the wall and into the kitchen as I usually do, but as I ran around I suddenly felt something biting me on the back of my neck. Come and have a look and see if you can see anything."

Scratch scuttled across to Whiskers and, using his front paws, parts the fur on the back of his neck.

He notices that something is moving under his fur. "Ugh, what's that he cries.

Snitch scuttles across to see if he can see what it is, "it looks like you've got fleas." he exclaims

"What me," cries Whiskers, "We never have fleas at this time of year. We got rid of them all last winter."

"Well, it looks as though you do now," says Snitch. "Lets see if we can get them off you.".

Snitch tries to pick the fleas off Whiskers back, managing to get one or two. As he picks them off he throws them on the floor and stamps on them.

Unfortunately one of the fleas escapes Snitch's paw and jumps onto his fur.

"Oooh, I think I might have one now" shouts Snitch, "Urgh! I can feel it crawling up my neck.

Soon Snitch is scratching. It seems there are definitely more than just a few fleas.

Within minutes all three rats are scratching. They scratch and scratch and scratch, and there is fur flying everywhere.

They try rolling in the dust to get rid of them, they try

The Tailors Cottage - Eloise (age 10)

picking them off each other, they even try getting wet in one of the puddles in the graveyard, which is one thing these rats hate!

Nothing they do seems to get rid of the itching - the fleas seem to be multiplying, and they are becoming infested with fleas.

"Where on earth did all these fleas come from?",

asks Snitch, "These are really horrible and viscous ones." When we've has fleas before, they haven't bitten as much as these do."

"I wonder if other rats in the village have them," asks Snitch? "I will see if I can find out next time out looking for food."

"Be careful," says Scratch, "don't forget the trouble you by had at the stocks when you met those other rats."

"Is there anything different in the tailor's cottage?", asks Snitch

"There are some old clothes or cloth in front of the fire that weren't there yesterday when I went looking for food," says Whiskers

"I saw a bundle of clothes taken from a cart that had come up from London," says Snitch, "maybe that's where they have come from."

"Do you think the fleas were in the old clothes?", Scratch asks.

"Maybe" said Snitch."Wherever they have come from, I wish they would go back. These fleas are driving me crazy."

The three rats continues scratching; there is fur flying everywhere. By the end of the day, they all look very scruffy and are very tired.

A Fateful Day

October 1665

The village is usually a bustling place, but it becomes eerily quiet one morning. Rather than villagers walking up and down the village streets as they usually do - there is no-one around. The church bell tolls slowly all of the day.

Whiskers goes out on his daily route to scavenge for food - after a few minutes though, he comes scuttling back into the log.

"What's wrong/, what's happening in the village?" Asks Snitch

"I don't know," says Whiskers, "there's no-one around and it definitely smells very different."

"You can smell that too," asks Scratch, "I thought it was just me."

"No, there is something very wrong," says Whiskers, "I'm going to go out again to see if I can

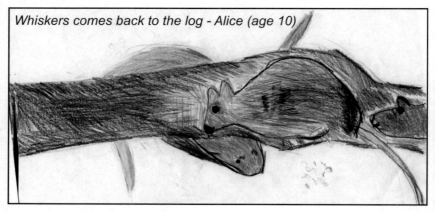
Whiskers comes back to the log - Alice (age 10)

find out what's happening."

Whiskers cautiously creeps out of the log and dashes from gravestone to gravestone until he gets to the church gate where he quickly looks up and down the road.

Nothing is moving, the wind is blowing grass and twigs along the road, and it is very quiet.

He scampers out of the gate and along the road to a row of cottages by the churchyard. He keeps close to the wall to be out of the sight of anyone.

Outside one of the cottages, owned by the village tailor, is a cart with a white bundle of cloth on it. The cloth has red bloodstains on it.

As Whiskers gets closer, he notices a hand sticking out of the edge of the cloth bundle. "There must be a body on the cart," he thinks. "That's strange though as the family who lives in that cottage are only young, and it's usually only old people who die."

After a few minutes, a short, stocky man comes out

24

of the cottage - he has a cloth wrapped around his face covering his mouth and nose and thick gloves on his hands. He moves slowly to the cart and pushes the hand back into the bundle of cloth.

At the cottage door, a woman and two children are crying and wailing. The woman puts her arms around the children and tries to calm them down, but it is no use, they cling on to their mothers' apron, they cry "don't take Daddy away"..

The man gets on the cart, and shouts to the horse to giddy up, he waves to the woman, and heads off slowly up the road. The woman at the door slowly turns, gathers her children, and goes back into the house.

Whiskers follows the cart as fast as he can, always trying to keep out of sight. The cart is only going slowly, but it still means Whiskers has to run as fast as he can to keep up.

At the edge of the village, the cart driver jumps off, gives the horse a nosebag of food, takes a spade from the back of the cart, and starts digging a hole in a field.

Whiskers runs quickly round to the front of the horse. He knows that there will be something to eat as grain always leaks out of the horse's nosebag.

He gobbles up what has dropped on the floor and saves some in his cheeks to take back for his friends.

He watches as the man digs the hole deeper and deeper. The pile of the earth by the side of the hole is growing larger and larger.

He keeps on digging until Whiskers can't see the man's head anymore. Finally, the man climbs out of the hole and calls over to someone working in a nearby field, "Hey John, give me a hand with this body."

The two men pick up the bundle of cloth with the body in it and throw it into the hole. "God save his soul," says the man as he takes off his hat and bows slightly.

Both men start to fill in the hole. It seems to take them forever as the hole is so deep.

Whiskers has seen similar activity before in the churchyard, but never a hole this deep and never out in the fields - he wonders what's happening.

When the cart driver and John have finished, they wash their hands in the spring by the side of the track. The cart driver thanks John, he gets back on his cart to ride back into the village.

"It looks as though you're going to have a busy time," says John

"Yes," says the cart driver, "It looks as though the pestilence is upon us."

When the cart and John are out of sight, Whiskers goes up to where the mound of earth has been left and smells the air - it smells strongly of death - more so than ever before.

"There is something terrible happening here," he says to himself as he heads back to the graveyard.

Once he gets back to the log, he says to the others, "There is something awful happening in the village, I have just watched them bury a body in a field outside the village. I have never seen them do that before and the smell of death is so strong up there."

"They usually bury bodies in the graveyard don't they?," Asks Snitch, "I wonder why they are doing things differently?"

"I don't know," says Whiskers, "but I don't like it."

On the Hunt for Food

To a rat, a small hole is like a door.
Saint Helena (AD 300)

November 1665

After the hot summer, the temperature drops, and the smell of death starts to fade.

The village starts to get back to normal with people out and about, fewer bodies are being buried, and things start to feel as it did. The cold weather seems to calm everything down.

The rats have survived the summer, although they look very scruffy with all the scratching they have been doing. The fleas have stayed with them all summer long.

They had tried everything they can to get rid of them, but nothing they do seems to get rid of them. So they carry on scratching day after day.

They have also endured being chased by the villagers who are blaming anything and everything for the disease.

"I am glad that the hot weather is over," says Snitch, "It is causing people to go mad, running around shouting and screaming."

"What's worse is that the water has stopped running in the troughs," says Whiskers, "People are having to try and catch rainwater to drink - it's a good job there are puddles for us to drink from around the graveyard."

There is a heavy frost in the mornings which makes the fields looked pretty as the early morning sun shines on them.

The rats look out of the log one morning; the frost on the gravestones twinkles in the sunlight.

"I like this time of year," says Scratch, "things get a lot quieter in the village when it's cold."

Snitch says, "I prefer the spring when all the flowers start to come out, and there are plenty of seeds to eat."

Whiskers say, "I think autumn is my favourite as we can collect nuts and seeds and store them for the winter. There are not as many cats around as they prefer to be next to the fire when it's cold."

"There aren't as many cats around in the village anyway," says Snitch," Many of the houses where people have died have had cats living there.
The villagers are not sure what is causing the disease, so they are grasping at any idea. They

think it might be the cats that are spreading the disease, so they are being killed; there are only a few left that have managed to escape to the fields around the village.

"I'm going to explore further up the village today," says Snitch, "It's a long time since I went to see what is happening at the other end of the village."

"Be careful," says Whiskers, "I know it's a bit quieter now, and there aren't as many cats, but people are still scared and there are the other rats up by the stocks."

There has been a light covering of powdery snow on the ground from the night before.

Snitch sniffs the air outside the log to see if it's safe and he puts one paw on the snow to see how deep it is. "Its not too deep so it should be OK"

He feels everything should be OK, so he carefully runs through the graveyard, scuttling from gravestone to gravestone, and pauses by the gateway onto the road.

He quickly jumps back behind the wall as someone with a strange beak-like mask and a dark

The Plague Doctor - Lucy (age 9)

cloak walks past shouting, "Only one death today' praise be, the pestilence seems to be over."

Snitch scampers up the village once the stranger has passed down the road, keeping close to the wall. As he passes the houses, he notices that some are empty and have black crosses daubed in paint on the doors.

"That's strange," he says to himself. "I have not seen those crosses before."

He returns to the log to tell the other rats what he has seen.

"The village is very quiet, and there are houses with black crosses on the door," Snitch says, "I think they must be the ones where people have died"

"We need to keep away from those then," says Snitch, "there will be disease in there."

"I agree," says Scratch, "I think we need to look for food out in the fields away from the village."

"But there's snow on the ground," says Whiskers, "it will be hard to find food in the fields; we will need to hunt for food in the village."

"That's going to be dangerous though, with the disease and the desperate villagers," says Snitch.

"Well, it will be that or starve," says Whiskers.

They agree that they will have to be careful if they

are going to forage in the village and try and find food at the edges of the fields which have been sheltered from the snow.

The Long Cold Winter

December/January 1666

The cold winter months have been hard for the rats. They have managed to store some food and there are still some berries on the trees.

They spend a lot of the time huddling in their log in the graveyard, sleeping, scratching and grooming.

Snitch yawns and stretches and says "we need to head out and find some food today as our food store is running low"

"Yes" says Whiskers, "If this cold weather goes on for much longer we will starve to death and end up having to eating each other!"

"Well, Snitch, you're the biggest and fattest so you will be the first one to go" says Scratch.

"But I am all muscle and gristle so I'll be a bit tough to chew on" says Snitch with a grin.

The three rats move to the opening in the log and sniff the air to see of there is danger around.

"All clear" declares Snitch, "Lets head to the mine to-day and see if there's any food there".

"Good Idea" Scratch agrees.

The rats take a few tentative steps in the snow to see how deep it is.

"Ugh its nearly up to my belly" cries Whiskers.

"Well its a good job your belly isn't big as you will be dragging it in the snow" laughs Snitch.

They scuttle out of the graveyard and along the path to the lead mine. They can hear the miners talking and laughing.

"They will be having a break" whispers Whiskers, "That's good as they might leave some scraps of food".

The rats wait for the miners to finish and go back to work. They scamper up to where the miners have been and run up the table leg.

On the table are lots of plates and cups.

"Over here", shouts Whiskers, "there's nearly a whole apple here".

"There's meat on this plate" says Scratch excitedly.

The rats sit there for a few minutes gorging themselves when suddenly a rock flies past Snitch's head and lands with a thump on the table beside him.

"Clear off you miserable rats" shouts one of the miners and he throws another stone at them.

The rats grab what food they can and run back down the table leg and along the path to the graveyard.

When they got back to the log they look at what food they had managed to scavenge and Snitch says "Well, this will keep us going for a few days at least".

After the trip in the snow they are cold, wet and tired and curl up at the back of the rotten log and after a few minutes fall fast asleep.

The Days of Death

June 1666

The long cold winter has been hard for everyone in the village as well as for the rats. Although there has only been a few deaths over the winter months.

The lead miners in the village are back hard at work after the cold winter months and heavy rain. The melting snow and rain had created a lot of flood water which had flooded some of the mines claiming the life of several of the miners.

The summer, however, brings hot weather and bright blue skies.

As the weather got hotter, the rats notice that there are more and more crosses on the houses and people being buried all over the place, in gardens and the fields around the village.

There is a constant sound of people crying and wailing all over the village, and the church bell seems to never stop tolling.

No one seems to knows what is causes the deaths, and there is panic throughout the village. Some people believe it is witchcraft; others think it is judgment from God.

There has been word from London that there is plague all over that city and many other towns. Stories of how people are trying to protect themselves also arrive in the village.

The villagers are walking around with strange coverings on their faces; some have bunches of flowers under their nose, others have smouldering bundles of grass and sticks hung around their necks, anything to try and keep the disease away.

The rats, however, are going about their normal day-to-day business, and there seems to be more food about than usual for this time of year.

The fleas are still bothering them, though, and they don't seem to be able to get rid of them whatever they do.

One morning when Snitch goes out looking for food, he notices the smell of death is stronger than it has ever been. He scuttles out of the graveyard into the street outside the church and sees there are bodies lying in the street. The situation is clearly getting worse.

He runs back to the log and tells the others what he has seen, "There are bodies all over the place, people are crying and moaning - no-one seems to know what to do."

"There's a really large man dragging the bodies out of the village to bury them," says Snitch. "Everyone is keeping well away from him, but he seems to be just getting on with the job of burying people."

"Maybe we should leave here," says Whiskers. "I saw today that the villagers are killing pigeons now. They seem to think they may be the ones carrying the disease; it won't be long before they start on us."

Scratch agrees, but Snitch says, "what if it is US that is causing the disease? If we went away we would just take it with us and spread it further. I think we should stay."

Scratch says that he saw men boarding up the church so no one can get in, and the preacher is telling people not to go out of the village or let anyone in.

"They have put extra guards on the Lydgate path into the village."

After a lot of discussions, the rats all agree that staying would probably be the best thing.

"If we're going to stay, we will have to think about where we get food from. In case it's the food that the villagers are eating that is poisoned - maybe we should stick to foraging for food in the fields and hedges rather than stealing it from the houses," Whiskers states.

The boarded up church - Isaac (age 11)

They agree this would be the best idea.

"The villagers are getting food from out on the boundary stones around the village," Snitch says. "We will sneak up there early in the morning and see if there are any scraps."

"It's a long way to go," says Whiskers

"Yes, but it will be safer than risking getting food from the diseased houses," Snitch commented.

They decide to give it a try and rather than wait for the morning they head out to the boundary stone when it gets dark to see if there is anything there to eat.

Whiskers says, "If there isn't anything at the boundary, stone, we can still look for nuts and seeds in the small wood on the way back".."

The three rats sniffed the air and peaked out of the log. Everything seems good. Carefully they scamper through the graveyard, stopping every now and then to look for any cats or dogs that might still be around.

Quickly this way", Snitch whispers as he looks back at the other two rats. Unfortunately, he lost concentration and tripped over his enormous feet. "Ouch," he shouts.

,
"Quiet," says Whiskers, "you'll let everyone know we are here and then we will be in trouble.

The rats scuttle down the road and head up towards the Lydgate which leads to the Boundary Stone on the hill overlooking Stony Middleton.

As they approach the Lydgate, Snitch, who is out in front, stops quickly, and the other two rats crash into his bottom.

"What did you do that for?", asks Whiskers

"There's something happening a little further up the lane," says Snitch, "It looks like they're burying another body."

The rats crouch by the wall at the bottom of the track and wait for the burial to finish.

"When the cold weather came, everyone thinks that the worse has passed, but clearly it hasn't, "says Scratch. "There still seems to be lots of people dying around the village."

"Yes, it looks like it's not over yet," says Snitch

When the people have gone from the burial area, the rats scamper past the grave.

"I get the strong smell of death again," says Whiskers.

"Yes" say the other two rats "It seems to be everywhere"

They continued through the fields to the boundary stone. This is a rock that has holes cut in the top, which villagers fill with vinegar to disinfect coins that are left in exchange for food.

Snitch sniffed the air as they got closer, "I can smell something - I hope it's food."

Whiskers scampers around the Boundary Stone and finds a bag with some bread in it. He starts nibbling at the bag and, after a few minutes, gnaws a hole that is big enough for the rats to get at the bread inside.

"Mm-mm this is good fresh bread," says Scratch with a mouthful of bread

Suddenly they hear footsteps and look around just in time as one of the villagers throws a stone.

"Go and get the rats," the villager shouts to his dog.

The three rats grab a piece of bread each and run for their lives into a rabbit hole on the side of the hill by the side of the boundary stone.

The rats go as deep as they can into a rabbit hole and huddle together.

"Go on, go and get the rats," the villager shouts to his dog.

The dog snarls and follows them, and stands at the entrance to the rabbit hole. The dog barks and barks and tries to scratch to make the hole wider with its paws.

The rats press themselves against the back wall of the rabbit hole as one of the villagers pushes his hand in to see if he can grab one of the rats.

"Go on, bite him", says Whiskers, I dare you!"

Snitch carefully crawls forward, making sure not to get too close to the grubby fingers; he takes a lunge and sinks his teeth into the villagers thumb.

At the boundary stone - Jude (age 10)

"Owwww, shouts the villager as he pulls his hand out of the hole with blood dripping from his thumb.

"We'll get them for this", says one of the other villagers as he wraps an old handkerchief round the hand and thumb.

The three rats huddle in the rabbit hold, shivering with fright.

"I hope they go away soon", cries Scratch

The Chase

"The clever cat eats cheese and breathes down rat holes with baited breath." W.C.Fields

June 1666

After what seemed like an age, the barking stops. Everything goes quiet and still.

"Do you think that the dog has gone" asks Snitch?

"I don't know," whispers Whiskers, "I think we should wait to see if it stays quiet."

The rats huddle together to try to stay warm. They wait and wait. There is no noise, but Snitch says, "I think we should stay here tonight and wait till its light in the morning before we go to venture out."

As the morning came and the birdsong wakes the rats, they stretch as much as they can in the dark rabbit hole and, after a bout of scratching and yawning, decide that one of them should go and see if the coast is clear.

"There's still no noise - I will go and see if I can see anything," says Snitch.

Slowly Snitch creeps towards the entrance to the rabbit hole.

"Be careful," whispers Scratch, "The dog might just be waiting for us to escape."

Snitch edges up the rabbit hole and sniffs the air to see if he can smell if the dog is still there. He can't smell anything bad, so he continues up towards the light at the end of the hole.

As he gets closer to the entrance, he stops and listens to see if he can hear anything. All is quiet. He sniffs the air again.

He carefully crawls towards the entrance and tentatively peaks out of the hole. He looks around but can't see the villagers or the dog.

'It seems to be all clear," he shouts back to the other two rats at the back of the rabbit hole.

The other two rats slowly head toward the light at the entrance - they make their way out carefully.

As the three rats emerge from the rabbit hole, they all sniff the air and have a good look around to check if there is any danger nearby. They start to head across the fields on their the way home.

As they reach a clump of trees, they all stop. They

hear a group of villagers coming towards the trees. They quickly dart into the undergrowth and look for somewhere to hide.

"Quickly this way," shouts Snitch as he runs behind a big fallen tree.

"Listen," whispers Scratch, "they seem to be shouting."

There are four villagers and their dogs heading up the path. "I saw the rats up here by the boundary stone yesterday; they are trying to steal our food," the first villager shouts.

"I've seen them around the graveyard and the stocks," says the second villager "maybe that's where they are coming from."

"Let's see if they're still around here; if not, we'll put poison down around the village that will sort them out," the third villager says. "We can't have them stealing our food."

The three rats cower behind the tree - not daring to breathe in case they are heard.

The dogs are let off their leads and started sniffing round along the path. One of the dogs heads into the clump of trees towards where the rats are hiding.

"What shall we do?" asks Whiskers

"I think we are going to have to run for it," says

Snitch, and he sets off at a fast pace through the undergrowth.

The other two rats follow as close as they can. Because he is a bigger rat, it is hard for them to keep up, but a dog's bark from behind spurs them on.

Suddenly the dog that has been sniffing in the wood seems to find their scent, and with its head down and tail pointing, he starts snuffling along the path the rats have run.

"Quickly," shouts Snitch, "It looks as though the dog is on to us."

The rats weave their way around the trees and through the undergrowth with the dog hot on their heals.

"How much further?," pants Scratch.

"We need to find somewhere where the dogs can't find us," says Whiskers.

"Let's see if we can find some water as the dogs will lose the scent in that," says Snitch.

The three rats keep on running and finally find a small stream running through a field. They dive in the water and swim downstream for a few minutes and finally pause puffing and panting at the edge of the stream. They make sure they stay in the water to hide their scent from the dogs.

They take a sneaky look back and see the dog running up and down the bank, trying to find the scent: the four villagers and the other dogs run up to the edge of the stream.

"Where are the rat's boy?," The first villager says to his dog. The dog carries on running up and down the stream edge barking.

"It's no good," shouts the second villager, "we have lost them."

"Let's go and lay some poison in the graveyard and by the stocks, that will stop them stealing our food," says the first Villager. The four villagers head back towards the village, followed by their dogs.

The rats wait until they can't see the villagers anymore, and they haul themselves up onto the bank of the stream.

"That was close!," Whiskers pants. "I have never had to run for my life before, and I never want to do it again."

The two other rats agree, and they shake themselves to get rid of the water. They huddle down together to try to warm up.

After some time, Snitch says, "I think it's time we should head back."

The three rats set off back towards the village and their log.

The Feast

July 1666

Over the next few months, the situation in the village gets worse, and the number of people dying seems to be increasing.

Life in the graveyard gets more dangerous as the villagers keep coming to see if they can find where the rats are living.

The rats only venture out in the very early morning or late at night so there is less chance of being caught.

There is plenty of seeds and nuts in the hedgerows, so the rats have got fat, although they are still being bothered by the fleas.

Whiskers says one morning, "I wonder how much longer the disease will last, I don't think there are that many people left in the village now."

"There are so many houses that are empty, and the village is very quiet," says Scratch.

There is more food for the rats though, and the

villagers that are left don't eat all the food that is left for them at the boundary stone, which means that the rats can sometimes have a feast.

On a hot summers morning, the rats decide to venture out to the boundary stone again to see if the villagers have left any food. They scamper through the graveyard and out towards the boundary stone.

When they get there, they notice that there is quite a lot of food there, and it is starting to rot.

"What's happening here," asked Whiskers, "why hasn't anybody been up to collect the food?"

"I don't know," says Snitch," gnawing on a large carrot, "but I'm glad they haven't."

The rats spend the rest of the day at the boundary stone eating and resting - constantly looking out for villagers, but none ever appear.

As the light starts to fade, the rats make their way back towards the village when they suddenly stop in their tracks. Across the path is the body of a man which hadn't been there when the went up earlier.

The body is blocking the path completely, and on the other side of the body there area group of villagers talking about what to do with it.

Nobody seemed to want to go past the body or move it. There is lots of shouting and arguing about what should be done.

"Where is Marshall Howe?" One of the villager's shouts, "he's the man who moves these bodies."

"His wife died yesterday, and he is still mourning for her, he had to bury her yesterday, and he hasn't been out of the house since," says one of the other villagers.

"But what about getting our food?" Shouts a woman from the back of the crowd, "we need to clear the path to the boundary stone, or we will starve."

The villagers finally decided that someone should be sent to fetch Marshall Howe and plead with him to move the body from the path.

After some time, the giant of a man slowly walks up to where the villagers are standing, shovel in one hand and a rope in the other. He didn't have his usual confident air.

The rats watch as Marshall digs a grave at the side of the path, puts a rope around the body, and drags it into the grave. A huge cheer goes up from the crowd of villagers as he fills in the grave.

"That's interesting," says Scratch, "the villagers are really scared of the disease."

"They are going to be really cross when they get to the boundary stone and find that we have eaten all their food," says Whiskers.

The villagers run past the rats, jumping over where

the body had been. They are desperate to get to the boundary stone and their food.

"Let's get out of here quickly," says Snitch, "they are going to be looking for who ate everything, and they are going to be very angry!"

"I think we should stick to our fields for the next few days and keep out of the way of the village," says Scratch

Rats in the Graveyard
Cerys (age 10)

The Attack

August 1666

It is a hot summers day, the birds are singing, and all seems well in the rats world.

The villagers are still wailing and crying, and there seems to be a lot more deaths in the village as the weather is getting hotter and hotter.

The rats notice that there are very few scraps of food in the village and little at the boundary stone, so they have taken to foraging in the fields around the village more often.

The rats keep very busy and have gathered nuts and seeds, which are plentiful at this time of year. They have built up quite a stock which they keep in the log for the winter months.

"We are going to have a good stockpile for the winter," says Snitch.

"Yes, there seems to be lots of seeds, berries, and nuts this year, more than I've ever seen before," says Whiskers.

"Maybe it's because the villagers are not collecting them like they normally do," says Snitch.

"They all seem to be worrying about where the disease is coming from," says Scratch, "and not going out looking for food but depending on the other villages leaving it at the boundary stones and wells."

Whiskers starts scratching behind his ear

"Do you think that the fleas are in our log?" Asked Scratch' "They seem to be more viscous when we are in there"?

Rats on their log - Poppy (age 10)

"It could be," says Whiskers, "As the weather is fine, let's move out to the other side of the graveyard - there is a nice pile of grass there which will keep us warm."

"Shall we move our food store'' asked Snitch, "We don't want anyone else to steal it."

"Good idea," says Scratch, "But it will take us quite a time to do it."

The rats decide that if they pile the seeds and nuts on a large leaf, it will be quicker to move their stash of food. So Whiskers goes off hunting for the biggest leaf he can find.

After looking all over the graveyard Whiskers comes across a large leaf which is bigger than him. He heads back to the rotten log dragging it behind him. "I hope this will be big enough," he says as he puffs and pants.

"Well its better than nothing," says Scratch, "Let's pile things on and see if it will work"

The rats carefully pile nearly all their nuts and seeds on the leaf, carefully stacking them with the bigger nuts around the outside and the seeds piled in the middle.

Snitch, who is the biggest rat, takes the stem of the leaf in his mouth and, walking backward, slowly pulls the heavy leaf with all the seeds and nuts along the ground towards the pile of grass they are going to use as their new home.

Just as they reach halfway Scratch hears a rustling behind them.

Suddenly a group of five scruffy-looking rats appear from behind one of the gravestones and start attacking the rats.

"Watch out," shouts Whiskers, as he tries to fend off the attackers by bearing his teeth and standing up on his back legs to make himself look bigger.

Snitch carries on pulling the leaf as fast as he can, but the attacking rats are faster and more numerous than the graveyard rats.

There is a real battle between all the rats, but in the end, Snitch is just left with the stalk of the leaf in his mouth, and the other two are lying on the ground bleeding.

The attacking rats have stolen all the graveyard rats' food. Scratch has a big wound on his back where one of the rats bit him. Whiskers has a badly injured paw that has been squashed.

"Where did they come from?," Asks Whiskers as he licks his paw and limps towards a pile of grass to hide and recover.

"I think they are the ones that attacked me by the stocks," says Snitch.

"Well, I think we need to think carefully about where are going to live as I am sure they will be back," says Whiskers.

"And we will need to stock up on more food for the winter," Scratch says as he helps Whiskers to the pile of grass.

"Yes, we are definitely going to need food for the winter," Snitch commented, "as we can't rely on scraps from the villagers."

The three rats arrange themselves and snuggle down for a well-deserved sleep hoping that the marauding rats won't disturb them again.

As daylight breaks and the sun shines into the grass pile, they stretch and yawn and smell the air. Other than the lingering smell of death, they can't sense that there are other rats around.

Snitch nervously peaks out of the pile of grass. He sniffs the air and looks around. Everything seems to be clear.

"It looks alright in the graveyard this morning," says Snitch. "Let's go looking for a safer place to live today and find somewhere where the other rats won't be able to find us."

"Great idea," says Whiskers licking his paw, which is still hurting

Snitch looks at Scratch's back and licks some of the blood off to see how bad the injury is. "It doesn't look too bad" he says, "It will soon heal".

The rats head off out of the graveyard to look for a new home. Snitch leads the way as he is the biggest rat and the only one that hasn't been injured.

They wander in the fields behind the graveyard looking for somewhere suitable to set up home. They spend time some around the mine workings but, although there were usually scraps of food around from where the miners ate their meals, it is a dangerous place as there are lots of stray cats living there.

Finally after what seems like an age they find an old rabbit burrow in the side of one of the old spoil heaps from the mine. The heap hasn't been used for some time and is covered in grass. The rabbit hole is deep and warm and the grass has grown over the entrance so it should be well hidden.

"This seems an ideal spot" says Whiskers, "lets explore the area and see if we can find some food.

The rats spent the rest of the day foraging for food and start restocking their winter larder.

Life in their New Home

There is nothing like staying at home for real comfort.
Jane Austen

September 1666

The rats forage around the fields and woods for food every day and even venture to the boundary stone some days to see if there is any food left there.

They must be careful, though, as the villagers are very protective of their food sources, and the rats have been chased on more than one occasion.

This is one such occasion.

The rats make their way up to the boundary stone in the early hours of the morning. At the stone they find a sack of vegetables that have been left and manage to nibble through the cloth of the sack to get inside.

Unfortunately, they were are so busy nibbling the vegetables that they forgot to keep a lookout, and a group of villagers are coming up the path from the village.

Quickly says Snitch, there are villagers coming and if they find us here we will be in great trouble.

This time they know where the rabbit hole is, so they quickly dash there to hide until the coast is clear.

The villagers reach the boundary stone and cant believe that something has eaten through the sack and managed to eat a lot of the vegetables that are inside.

"I bet its those damn rats again" says one of the villagers.

"I thought they had put poison down in the graveyard to kill them off" says another.

"Well it has clearly not worked" says a third.

The villagers grab what is left of the food and head slowly back down towards the village - vowing to make sure the rats are finally got rid of.

When the coast seems to be clear the rats head back down the path into the village, they are very careful and either run through the undergrowth or are keep very close to walls so they are not seen or heard.

As they approach the Main Street, the rats pause and sniff the air. There is something different. It wasn't the strong smell of death that they have smelt before - this is something strange.

They keep pausing to sniff the air, and Snitch says, "there is something wrong; I don't like that smell."

"I think I have smelt something like that before," says Whiskers "it was just before we found that old rabbit, Fluffy, dead by one of the graves."

They turn into the churchyard past the church and headed towards their rabbit hole.

Scratch stops and says, "It looks like someone has left us some food over there; let's go and have a look."

"Be careful," says Whiskers, "remember Fluffy - I think it might be a trap, the villagers would not leave us food for no reason, don't forget they are short of food themselves.

The rats move slowly away from the pile of food and towards their old home in the rotten log.

"It looks like someone has blocked up the entrance to our old home, and look, there's another pile of food," says Scratch. "That food looks really tasty, and I am so hungry."

"Keep away from it," shouts Snitch, "I think it might be poisoned."

Whiskers quickly moves to the front of the rats and holds his paws up, "Let's get away from here and back to the safety of our rabbit hole as it looks like it is going to be a cold night again," says Whiskers.

Scratch leads the way as they head out of the back of the graveyard and to their rabbit hole.

"If the Villagers are trying to poison us, it won't be long before they find our new home," says Scratch, "I think we should look for somewhere safer."

"I agree," says Snitch, "Let's head out tomorrow and find somewhere away from the village and all the people."

In the early morning they walk and walk until they find an old haystack on the edge of a field.

Snitch runs round the outside of the haystack and shouts, "There's a hole here between the sheaves which we can get in and shelter from the wind and cold," he says.

The other two rats head to where they think they can hear Snitch's voice. They head in and find Snitch in a small space where they can all huddle together and hopefully will be safe from predators and the weather.

They curl up and settle down for a good night's sleep.

Early the next morning the rats venture out of the haystack and sniff the air for any danger. It seems safe so they decide to go down to the village to see what is happening.

The village is a very different place now. It is over a year since the first death at the tailor's cottage when the rats had their first smell of death.

This smell wasn't as strong as it has been, and the rats start to go carefully back into the village to try and find any scraps of food.

Many of the houses are empty, and these are good places to hunt for food as lots have been left lying around when villagers have died.

The pestilence has taken mainly men, and this means that the women of the village have taken on many of their tasks, such as ploughing the fields and planting seeds.

The church finally reopens its doors, and singing can be heard on a warm Sunday morning as the rats head down to their original home to see if they can get back in.

The smell of the poison seems to have gone, and the heavy rain and frost has moved the earth and rocks that have been piled in front of the entrance by the villagers.

"Come on, let's see if we can get back into our old home," shouts Snitch as he claws away at some of the earth to clear the entrance.

"Are you sure?", Asked Whiskers, "don't forget the villagers are trying to kill us."

Snitch pulls at the twigs that are blocking up the

entrance to the log.

"It smells alright to me," says Scratch as he follows Snitch into the old log.

The three rats scurry around their old home.

"It looks as though we have never left," says Whiskers.

"Yes," says Snitch; your area is untidy as ever.

"Nothing new there then," says Scratch

The rats spend time tidying up their home, but it doesn't feel quite right. There are still memories of all the death and particularly the chase from the boundary stone.

"I'm not sure I want to stay here," says Snitch as he scuttles round the old log. "I enjoy being out in the fields with the fresh air."

"Me too," says Whiskers, "Maybe we need to be country rats rather than village rats."

"I don't agree," says Scratch," I like being in the village; there's always different kinds of food and not just nuts and seeds."

"Always thinking about your stomach," says Snitch.

The rats agree that they should stay in the graveyard in the Summer and haystack in the Winter as it is warmer, and hopefully their stack of food will be safer there. They decide to make sure they have a store of food in more than one place though in case they get raided again.

Payback

October 1666

As summer turns to autumn and the weather gets colder, the rats head back to the haystack. They start looking for food in the hedgerows.

Snitch says," I'm going to have one last look at the stocks on the village green to see if there is any food there."

"Be careful," says Whiskers, "don't forget the last time you went up there and got chased by that other pack of rats".

"I am sure it will be OK" he says and Snitch heads off, making sure he stays in the undergrowth by the side of the road. As no-one had been cutting the verges there is plenty of cover for a rat.

When he arrives at the stocks and notices that there isn't any food for him to gather and he turns to head back down the village. As he turns there is a gust of wind and he gets a strange smell coming from the field next door to the stocks.

"I have sensed that smell before," he says to

himself.

"It smells like the poison that the villagers put down in the graveyard to try and kill us," he thinks,

He carefully creeps closer to where the smell is coming from, and as he does, he comes across a group of dead rats all lying round in a circle. In the middle of the ring is what's left of a pile of food.

Ugh, he thinks to himself, "that could have been us":

He carefully edges around the dead rats, making sure he doesn't touch the bodies or what's left of the food.

Snitch sees an entrance to a hole in the banking at the edge of the field behind the dead rats.

He carefully creeps towards the hole - sniffing the air all the time.

Looking into the hole, he is amazed at the pile of food that there is in front of him. It is the other rat's store for the winter.

He turns around, and quickly hurries back to the graveyard and breathlessly says to the other rats, "quickly, you won't believe what I have found, our store of food for the winter is going to be OK."

"What do you mean?": Asks Scratch

"You know the rats that stole all our winter supplies," says Snitch, "Well, they were so greedy that they

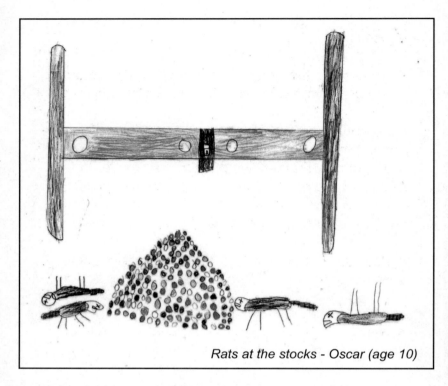

Rats at the stocks - Oscar (age 10)

ate the poisoned food that the villagers have put down for them, and would you believe it they have left their huge stock of winter food abandoned."

"Really," says Scratch, "I cant believe that they would be so stupid"

"Yes," says Snitch, "Let's go and bring it back for us."

The rats headed off towards the stocks and follow Snitch into the hole the rats have been using.

"I can't believe what I am seeing," says Scratch

"Well, believe me, it's true," says Snitch

The three rats gather what they can carry and start the first of many journeys to transport the food back to their two homes - making sure that there was food in both the places just in case.

As busy as they are, the rats still take most of the day to take all the seeds, nuts, and berries back. They carefully store it in neat piles so that they can enjoy it over the winter months.

When they are finished, they lay down in the rotten log and look at the great pile of food.

"That's going to keep us going for months if we're careful," says Whiskers

"And we have the other store in the log, so we should have food to take us well into the spring," says Scratch

"Let's hope that we don't get raided again," says Whiskers.

"Now that the other rats are dead, it unlikely," says Snitch

The three rats settle down for the night, knowing that they have enough food to last them for many months and that the villagers would probably not bother them as the disease seems to have passed.

Life in the village seemed to get back to normal, although nobody forgot the terrible months that the pestilence has had on the village. Many people have died, and those left struggle to survive in the early months after the disease left the village.

Life for the rats soon gets back to as normal as it can be, and as autumn turns to winter, they settle down to a good life in the haystack, knowing that they are safe - at least for the time being.

The end

St Lawrence Church - Honor (age 9)